Tree Wood

Four-Leaf Clover

Dearest MDB – You guide me on my path, day by day,
and with you by my side I can follow my dreams.
Thank you for putting the magic back into my life.
– S. F.

For Sarah and Alfred.
Lifting spirits and sharing dreams.
– S. W.

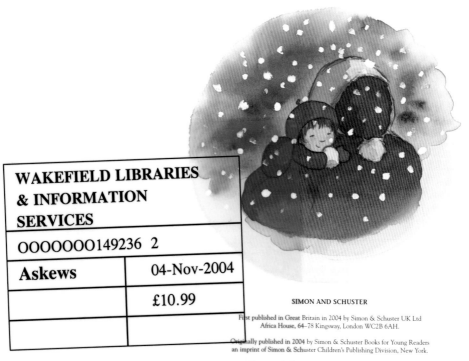

SIMON AND SCHUSTER

First published in Great Britain in 2004 by Simon & Schuster UK Ltd
Africa House, 64–78 Kingsway, London WC2B 6AH.

Originally published in 2004 by Simon & Schuster Books for Young Readers
an imprint of Simon & Schuster Children's Publishing Division, New York.

Text copyright © 2004 Sarah Ferguson, The Duchess of York.
Illustrations copyright © 2004 Sam Williams.

Book design by Lee Wade and David Bennett.
The text for this book is set in Goudy.
The illustrations for this book are rendered in soft pencil and watercolour on Arches paper.

A CIP catalogue record for this book is available from the British Library upon request.

ISBN 0-689-86072-2
Printed in the United States of America
1 3 5 7 9 10 8 6 4 2

Little Red's
Christmas Story

Sarah Ferguson
The Duchess of York

Illustrated by
Sam Williams

SIMON AND SCHUSTER

London   New York   Sydney

*I*t was Christmas Eve at Buttercup Cottage. The house was covered with snow, and long squiggly icicles dangled from the roof. Little Red and her friends were ready to set off for Christmas Tree Wood, where their favourite little fir tree grew.

"Let's get a wiggle on!" said Little Red. "It's time to go and we've got lots of presents to deliver along the way."

Singing carols, the merry gang crunched through the snow while snowflakes bustled all around.

In Purdey's Pasture, they stopped to give the mouse family some sugary cinnamon sticks.

Then they headed for Sansome's Meadow. Little Red had made some delicious treacle shortbread for the robins who lived there.

And their last stop was to call on the badgers in Four-Leaf Clover Field. "I made this acorn necklace for you, Mrs Badger," said Little Red proudly.

"And here's some of your favourite walnut fudge, Mr Badger." She held out a beautifully-wrapped bundle.

"Mmmm, thank you," said Mr Badger. "Now, where are you off to next?"

"We're going to find our tree, yippee!" yelled Little Blue with glee.

The four friends arrived at the edge of Christmas Tree Wood.

"Yippeedoodledan!" cried Little Blue, hopping from foot to foot and getting tangled in his scarf. He had just started to build an enormous snowman, when Roany gave a cough.

"Ahem!" she snorted as carrots spluttered from her mouth. "I hate to break up the seasonal silliness, but what's that light coming from behind the trees?"

"Whatever can it be?" wondered Little Blue.

"I think I know *who* it could be," laughed Little Red merrily as she skipped into the wood.

There, in a clearing, stood Father Christmas with his sleigh and his eight reindeer.

"How lovely to see you!" said Little Red.

"By jingle, by jolly, by jove!" chortled Father Christmas. "If it's not my dear friend, Little Red."

Little Blue, Roany and Gino all looked on in amazement. They had no idea that Little Red was one of Father Christmas's friends!

"I am in a bit of a tizzy, my dear," explained Father Christmas. "Poor Percy has a streaming cold, and he just can't go on any longer. I'll never be able to get all these presents delivered with only seven reindeer."

"I have an idea," said Little Red, looking gingerly at Roany.

"Oh, no!" said Roany, flicking her mane defiantly. "I'm sorry, but I can't fly and I *won't* fly."

As quick as a flash Little Red grabbed her sack of smiles and, before Roany could say 'jingle bells', she sprinkled magic flying dust all over the stubborn pony's hooves.

"Now you'll be able to fly!" announced Little Red triumphantly.

"We'll see about that," said a rather huffy Roany. "But if you're right, I'll expect an enormous bunch of carrots and a mountain of sugar lumps."

"Your problem's solved, Father Christmas," giggled Little Red as she kissed Roany's velvety nose. "I knew I could rely on you," she whispered.

"Ho, ho, ho!" laughed Father Christmas. "But time's running out and I'm still going to need some extra help. Could you come too, Little Red?"

"I think so," she answered.

Then she turned to Little Blue. "I know that Percy will be safe in your care . . . and Bear, too," said Little Red as she handed her beloved teddy to her friend. "He doesn't like heights, you see."

Little Red hurried along to take her place next to Father Christmas on the sleigh. "I promise to bring you back a present, Little Blue!" she called.

"Eyes forward!" whooped Father Christmas to the reindeer and Roany as the sleigh whizzed off into the night air.

As Roany's hooves left the ground, the carrot she was chewing dropped from her open mouth. "Christmas crackers!" she gasped. "I'm flying!"

A very downcast Little Blue, with a snuffly Percy and a grumpy Gino, waved a sad goodbye to Little Red. How Little Blue would have loved to fly on Father Christmas's sleigh! "I suppose we'd better go home," he sighed. "Gino, can you dig up our favourite tree to take back to Buttercup Cottage?" Gino threw Little Blue a disgruntled look as he dug the little tree out of the ground.

Little Blue loaded the tree onto the sledge, popping Bear on top. He struggled to lead Percy with one hand and pull the sledge with the other as they headed for home.

"Whooppee! Whizzing, whirling walnuts!" shrieked Little Red as the sleigh hurtled through the skies. But then a worried frown appeared on her forehead. "I do hope that Percy's feeling better, that Bear's all right, and that Little Blue remembers to hug them both," she said.

"There, there, don't despair. Your bear's in good care!" sang Father Christmas as they flew over the snowy rooftops.

It was late when Little Blue, Gino and Percy trudged up the path to Buttercup Cottage. They were all tired, cold and utterly fed up.

"Little Red has all the fun. I bet she forgets my present," muttered Little Blue as he dragged the fir tree through the front door. Curled up cosily in the armchair was Purdey. She bustled around, settling Percy by the fire and wrapping him in a blanket.

Then she brought him a hot-water bottle and carefully placed his hooves into a bucket of heated honeysuckle water.

Suddenly Little Blue's hair stood on end. "Dingly, dangly disasters and dog-eared doughnuts!" he cried. "Where's Bear?" Little Blue ran round and round in circles, getting more and more tangled in his scarf.

"He must have fallen off the sledge! Little Red will never forgive me," he shrieked. "I've got to find him." And with that, Little Blue tore out of the cottage.

He stumbled in the direction of Christmas Tree Wood, with tears streaming down his face. "I'm a hopeless friend," he whimpered. "I'm not just Little Blue, I'm very blue."

But just as he turned the corner into Sansome's Meadow, he met Mrs Badger trundling her wheelbarrow full of little badgers. Through his tears Little Blue noticed a small paw waving from the wheelbarrow. It wasn't a badger paw . . . it was Bear's paw!

"Oh, oh, oh, Mrs Badger, you've found Bear!" he cried, hugging and squeezing her with all his might.

"Yes, dear," said Mrs Badger. "I found him half-buried in the snow outside our house and recognised him straight away. I know how fond Little Red is of her bear so I thought I should return him, quick sticks!"

"Christmaspuddingtastic!" laughed Little Blue, and he wrapped Bear very carefully in his scarf. Then he told Mrs Badger all about Little Red's adventure. "Why don't you come back to Buttercup Cottage with us – you could help decorate the tree," he said.

"I'm all behind like Roany's tail, and we must finish before Little Red and Roany get back." So, with Bear tucked inside his scarf, Little Blue rushed back to Buttercup Cottage with Mrs Badger, all the baby badgers and Gino.

Everyone helped to decorate the Christmas tree . . . and the cottage . . . and even Percy's antlers. As they worked, they slurped marshmallow cocoa and crunched on crusty custard Christmas crumpets.

Suddenly Gino began barking excitedly and ran to the window. "Someone must be outside," said Little Blue as he undid the latch and opened the door, just as . . .

Little Red walked down the path, laden with presents. Roany was smirking smugly from ear to ear.

Little Red hugged and kissed each of her friends in turn. Then everyone looked to the sky and waved to Father Christmas as his sleigh flew up into the stars.

"Thank you for a wonderful adventure, Father Christmas. We'll send Percy back to you when he's quite, quite better," called Little Red.

"Come inside, Little Red. You must be frozen," fussed Mrs Badger.
"Yes, do hurry, Little Red," said Little Blue as he eagerly eyed the
pile of presents. Everyone followed him into Buttercup Cottage as he
pulled Little Red by the sleeve.

"How Christmassy everything looks! The tree is just beautiful!" gasped Little Red, hugging Bear close to her heart. "Little Blue," she said, handing him a very odd-shaped parcel, "this is for you. Thank you so much for looking after Percy and Bear. What a true friend you are!"

"A horn!" cried Little Blue. "Fantabuloso! Toot, toot! It's just the thing to make my tricycle go faster!"

"Ahem," sniffed Roany. "And what about my present?"

"Oh, Roany, you've been the biggest star in the universe!" said Little Red. "That's why Father Christmas wanted you to have these as an extra-special treat."

Roany's eyes sparkled as Little Red placed a bucket full of crunchy, candy-coated Christmas carrots in front of her. "It was a piece of Christmas carrot cake!" Roany chuckled.

Little Red raised her cup of marshmallow cocoa.
"Hurrah for Little Blue and hurrah for Roany!" she
laughed proudly.
"Hip hip hooray, we've all saved Christmas Day!"
everyone cheered.

HAPPY CHRISTMAS

The Village

Sansome's
Meadow

Buttercup Cottage

Purdey's Pasture

Lily Pad Pond